A.D. Wood

The Truth and the Wine Interest!

A.D. Wood

The Truth and the Wine Interest!

ISBN/EAN: 9783337325824

Printed in Europe, USA, Canada, Australia, Japan

Cover: Foto ©Andreas Hilbeck / pixelio.de

More available books at **www.hansebooks.com**

AND

The Wine Interest!

PROSPERITY OR PAUPERISM?

WILL WINE MAKING PAY?

A QUESTION OF FINANCE.

———

Published for the Grand Lodge, I. O. G. T.,
of California,

By CAPT. A. D. WOOD,

San Francisco.

———

THIRD EDITION.

———

SAN FRANCISCO:
BACON & COMPANY, PRINTERS.
1883.

THE TRUTH

THE WINE INTEREST.

There was a time not very long ago, when wine was almost universally believed to be a legitimate natural product of the fruits of the soil, and a proper article appointed by the Creator for the use of man. It was supposed to be nourishing, strengthening, supporting, and to possess a greater range and variety of medicinal properties than were ever claimed for Holloways Pills or R. V. Pierce's quackeries. It was also believed that the Creator had been a little careless or indiscreet or mistaken, in providing us with such a useful food and such a cure-all medicine, that is so expensive and so dangerous, and so tempting to abuse and excess; and which has destroyed more human lives and souls and properties, and caused more sin, crime, misery and untimely death than war, pestilence, famine and all the other evils combined that have ever cursed the world.

But there were some folks who did not believe the Creator ever made mistakes or surrounded men with snares of perdition; they subjected wine to a thoroly scientific inquisition. The result was the discovery that every pretension ever made for wine outside of the Bible and the writings of some heathen philosophers, was a fraud, a folly, a delusion: they found wine was an unmitigated impostor, a cheat, a lie, in every thing. It was and is just what the Bible says; a mocker, a disturber, a deceiver, a perverter, a biter, a stinger, a fell destroyer. Its claim to be nourishing, strengthening and a medicine was most absolutely false. Every thing the world had believed of it was a mistake, except that it was dangerous. It was found that God never made or provided for making a particle of it. It was and is a product of rotten grapes, after every particle of any useful property of the grape has been destroyed. It is nothing but alcohol, and water with a flavor which is unsubstantial, and a vestige of sugar perhaps. It can be made just as good from rotten potatoes or apples or cactus plants or cabbage leaves or molasses—and water, and a few coloring and flavoring drugs—provided always, that the original vegetable article from which it is made, must be rotted and putrified and made to emit for days a nauseous and deadly poisonous gas and a horrible stench.

The value put upon wine was a monstrous fraud too. The imitations of regular grape wine made from any alcoholic base at a few cents a gallon, are consumed all over the world by drinkers without suspicion, and they answer the purpose equally well. No one who buys French wines in or out of France, of the cheapest up to the most expensive brands, unless he has watched their manufacture, has the least security that they are not frauds made for 10 or 20 cents a gallon. No one, who drinks

California wine away from the ranch or factory where grape wine is made, knows or can find out whether. it is potato or grape or cider wine. Everybody who drinks it is quite satisfied of one thing: and that is all he needs or wants to know: it will make drunk, and one thing is actually as good as another for that purpose. There would be a terrible outcry made if tea and coffee merchants were known to sell a fabricated article for a dollar or two a pound, that they were manufacturing from old rotten rubbish at four or five cents a pound; but, as the scripture says, wine is a mocker and they that are entrapped by it are not wise. So one thing answers for them as well as another, if it has the right amount of drunk in it.

The advocates of the manufacture and sale of wine are so, either because they desire to make money themselves by the ruin of others—or they have been entrapped and mocked and fooled by wine—or they are most deplorably and comprehensively ignorant of everything that relates to wine as almost every wine drinker in this country is.

The traders in drunkenness and their tools have one defensive weapon, which they are very fond of using, because they have no other.

They say the advocates of sobriety and honesty and decency *lie* about wine and drink, to make money out of it someway. Now every body with any sense at all knows that such a charge is utterly false, because we are the only people in the country who could sell liquor and make money by it: not drinking ourselves, we could gobble up all the money of the drinkers and hold on to it, and only lose our self respect and character and honesty and our souls: we could hold on to the fool's money to the last, but the liquor sellers cannot: they drink and go to death and ruin and perdition, at a quicker average rate than the victims they destroy. If we were after money and would lie to get it, we could make easy fortunes in the wine business.

The wine dealers have no motive except gain, and that too, dishonest gain; gain obtained at the expense of their neighbor's life and soul and of their own. We have a prospective gain too, from the final extinction of wine; and we are proud of it. We expect to save 100.000 or so of lives from going out in darkness and in the service of satan every year in this country. We expect to be the helpers and instruments in making millions of homes and many millions of people happy, safe and joyous and prosperous thru the downfall of the devouring monster, who has been the merciless butcher of our race, the destroyer of our homes, the invader of our peace for centuries. We expect to see this now most unhappy of all States become a garden of innocence and peace and happiness and the worship of the God of our country replace the horrible orgies of satan which now desolate it. And we hope with good reason to see every nasty deadfall that now destroys all honest business, replaced with at least five honest and enriching industries and employments. And we hope many millions of people will dwell in Heaven who can never get there while the grogshop and the devil rule here.

The people who want to gain money by the drunkenness and ruin of their neighbors tell us, that making wine and brandy is an enriching business for the wine makers and for the State. It is freely admitted that if a remunerative price could be obtained for those drinks and they should all be exported and sold, and not a drop consumed in the State, the business would be as enriching to us here as any other could be, yielding the same percentage of advance upon cost. ,That is quite clear. But we know its purchase and use would result in a dead loss to its consumers abroad, without doing them a particle of benefit; we know it would kill thousands of men, women and children, and would have just the same effects as its use by the Alaska Indians, only those effects would be a little slower among some of the whites.

If we could steal a large amount of cattle and horses every year in Oregon and sell them in Nevada at an exorbitant profit without any risk of being caught and hung, we should get very rich all the same; but the people of Oregon and Nevada would be a good deal more impoverished than we should be enriched; and that is precisely what occurs with our wine and brandy customers, except that they are worse sufferers than people who only have their cattle stolen.

Our leading papers which fish for subscribers by prophesying smooth things and great wealth from the cultivation of drunkenness in this State, are very fond at times of enlarging upon the monstrous crime of England in forcing opium upon the Chinese. They have no subscribers in England or they would sing an entirely different song. The crime of England in that thing is one of the most wicked and cruel and sordid and utterly horrible ever known in the history of sin; but it is very much like our sending wine and brandy to China and Japan and England or anywhere. ˙ England dont force any body in China to buy opium a particle more than we force Englishmen to buy brandy. But she does compel the Chinese Emperor and his advisers to abstain from prohibiting its voluntary purchase by the Chinese people. That is all the difference and it is a very trifling one.

But the pretensions and promises and statistics and arguments of the wine and brandy advocates are utterly fallacious and unfounded. There are statements made by some of them which are so false that they seem designedly so; some false impressions are received and promulgated thru the terrible fanaticism enkindled by avarice and the use of these poison beverages, and no doubt in most instances the most sublimely ridiculous and self-contradictory statements are made and accepted and believed because of the benighted ignorance which is so very general upon the whole subject.

In next and following numbers these pretensions will be examined and their falsehood exposed.

NUMBER II.

There are two and only two classes of enemies to the grape growers; both equally hostile to their financial interests and to their comfort and welfare. One class is the phylloxera which seeks to destroy their vines root and branch: the other is the wine and brandy sharp who proposes to blast this magnificent, wholesome, worthy and profitable industry, to hoist over it the death's head and crossbones of the pirate flag, and prostitute the luscious clusters of the vine into a poisonous breath of hell for the destruction of men's lives and souls; to make the beautiful vineyard an instrument of devastation and beggary and death to the vine grower and to the victim of the poison cup.

There is no use in California for either the phylloxera or the other more costly and dangerous pest. If we are to have either, the former should be our choice: it only attacks the vine: it dont attack our lives and our homes and our morals. It dont build penitentiaries and lunatic asylums and flood them full all the time with human wrecks. The other pest does.

The vine grower has only one class of friends in this State to help him in this emergency, and of that class is the RESCUE and the Order of Good Templars. Let us talk it over and see who are friends and who are enemies of the vineyard men.

The temperance men have no possible personal gain to derive from the vineyard men: the wine and brandy men expect nothing but pecuniary gain and have only that motive: can have no other. We propose if possible to put a stop to the waste of your grapes at a cent or three-eights of a cent a pound which will probably soon be their price, to go into the rot heap and be turned into crazing, maddening, useless poison. We want to spoil that market of waste and drunkenness and shame and poverty if we can. But we offer you something vastly more profitable than that very uncertain market.

The production of raisins and the employment of
the boys and girls of the vine growers, in place of
the chinamen of the winery, can be made doubly
or trebly profitable as compared with the drunkery
process. But you say, raisins cannot be made everywhere. Well, green fruit can be raised everywhere, and with as much energy and effort and
State aid, expended in the development of the canned and preserved grape and grape juice, as has
been given to the wine and brandy interest, a much
more profitable and a perfectly safe and proper market can be secured for the fruit of the vine.

With fair dealing on the part of the railroad interest in place of their present system of charging
four or five times the lawful honest freight on fresh
fruit delivered in the East, a market can be secured
for 1000 tons of fresh grapes a day which should
give the grower three times the price paid by the
wine and brandy makers. But it is admitted that
kind of a business wont make the distillers millionaires by converting the vine growers into paupers
and peons, as may be found marked out on the tres-
tle board of the future, by the wine men.

There is no possible light in which the anti-bran-
dy men can be truthfully put, except as the friends
of the vine growers, and there is no possible light
in which the wine and brandy makers and their
newspaper advocates can truthfully appear, except
as their worst and most insidious enemies, just like
t' e phylloxera, but more far reaching in their prospective mischief.

It is readily admitted that if we come to you
with a request to let your grapes rot on the vines or

to dig up your vineyards, and engage in some less profitable industry, we should not expect a respectful hearing, however just and fair our case might be. But we commend you to safety and a future of prosperity and comfort. Our opponents will surely admit, as we do, that the manufacture of wine and brandy will be subject to about the same conditions here, as in other countries where it has been tried, in proportion to the extent to which the business has been carried.

If it has made any country richer, happier or more moral and honest, it is admitted, there is every reason to presume that the business will produce a similar result here. If it has benefited one-half or one-fourth or one-tenth of the countries that have harbored wine and brandy manufacture, it is admitted by us, that California has just that chance to be benefitted financially, morally and socially. And if it can be proved never to have in the slightest degree benefitted any country, it is fair to expect that it will act similarly here. If it can be proved that it never was anything but a destroying and debauching and pauperizing agency. in every other country, the asseverations and oaths of a million brandy distillers, reprobate newspaper time servers and saloonkeepers, will never make it have any other effect in this country; it will be shown that it never can nor could have any but an evil and damnable tendency in every possible direction.

There are two pictures offered to-day to the people of California. One drawn by any 'reasoning, commonsense observer and reader of the world's history, and the other by the devotee and dupe of the bottle and by those whom the greed of ill-gotten gain has blinded.

The picture which the sober reasoner sees, as the result of a plain common sense application of A. B. C. business principles to the grape culture question—is that of a million happy rural homes in this State, embowered in every beautiful embellishment of tree and flower and shrub and vine; every one of them fruitful in evidences of thrift and industry and taste, comfort and culture, on the part of the occupants. Every one a home of virtue and and peace and a nursery of American good citizenship. A paradise example to all the world of the proper employment of God's gifts and men's reasoning faculties.

The other picture, that whose outlines have been cast by the agents of the great mocker and tempter enemy of mankind, is one of bleak desolation, ruined homes, departed peace, the inevitable, ever present insignia of drunkenness, vice, debauchery, crime, and beggary and filthiness, interspersed with here and there a rare exception of fortunate exemption from the prevailing ruin.

The picture that shall be, will be the work of the grape growers themselves. They will elect to make their portions of the State nests of crime and ignorance and drunkenness and beggary—or homes of virtue, peace, sobriety and their inevitable fruits, health, wealth and happiness. What wine and brandy has done, it always will, where it exists. What it has done and is doing elsewhere will be detailed in following chapters.

NUMBER III

Some of the claims set up by the wine and brandy apostles are too silly and too self-evidently false to be noticed seriously: they are only believed by the hopelessly ignorant and unthinking. They say at one time, that the use of wine does not lead to drunkenness, at another, one kind of wine does, but the other does not: which is of course the most simple nonsense. Again they say that drunkenness is not prevalent in wine making countries, when they know that they have been little else than nurseries of drunkards, ever since the time of Noah, and are to-day the filthiest harlot civilizations of the world. They still keep rehearsing the old worn out folly, that the use of beer and wine or either diminishes the use of stronger liquors: whereas all experience has proved that they have the opposite tendency.

It has been claimed that the *pure* wines of this State were not seductive allurements to drunkenness, that they were conducive to sobriety. But every body who has had an opportunity of observation, knows the utter falsehood of the claim. Even Mr. Wetmore, one of the chief priests of the brandy idolatry, has of late publicly declared that a large portion of the wines of this State in common use, are unfit to be used and ought to be sent to the distillery. And no one will deny that the distillery is an unmistakable drunkard factory.

In England 50 years ago it was deemed by the crazy people who drink, that drunkenness could be supplanted by affording facilities for the sale of beer. Beer houses were opened everywhere to coax drinkers away from gin and whisky. Great results were expected and they came: drunkenness and debauchery were fearfully aggravated and the sale of the strong liquors vastly increased. Ever since, it has been admitted that the Beer Act was the most awful disaster that ever befel England. But a similar attempt was made about 25 years ago and carried out, to cure drunkenness in England by introducing cheap French wines, which resulted like introducing the small pox to supplant the yellow fever, and of course drunkenness aud the use of strong spirits both had a marked increase, as all sensible men had foreseen and declared.

Every one who can and wants to see, must know that scores of thousands become drinkers and drunkards thru drinking beer and wine, who never would have acquired a taste, or conquered their natural repugnance, for strong liquors had their been no lighter drink to begin with. No one has ever seen an instance of a free drinker of strong liquors becoming a moderate drinker of light wine or beer, or if one has been such an exception, he is one against ten thousand who have gone the other way.

But the most potent argument that falls upon the ear of the vineyardist, is the

WEALTH

To be derived from the wretched prostitution of the grape into brandy and fermented wine for the pauperization and destruction of others. Now there are quite a number of wine making countries

which should be brot forward as examples of the
enriching effects of turning good grapes into pauperizing drinks. First among these should be

SPAIN.

That country has drawn revenues enough from
its colonies to make it a country of rich bankers.
The people should have been rich and amazingly
prosperous from that source alone. The mines and
plunder from South America alone ought to have
made Spain a country of gold and silver. Its posi-
tion and climate and its own soil and seashore and
mines, should have made Spain rich without any
other resources. If wine and brandy could ever be
enriching, Spain has made enough of them to have
made her the Bank of Europe. But because of the
curse of her infernal wine traffic, her people and
her government are bankrupt and pauperized both
physically and morally. They drink nearly all the
wine they make, which is an utter waste of the industry and land employed in its production. With
every resource and opportunity for the most teem-
ing prosperity, her 16 million people are semi-bar-
barous—only one in 5 can read and write. About a
million of their nobility have almost or quite de-
generated to pauperism and a large proportion of the
people are paupers, beggars, brigands &c with no
redeeming qualities: the people and country exactly fill the bill of a drinking, dancing, gambling, la-
zy, dirty, debauched and utterly contemptible
played out nation of wine makers, and it was the
wine makers that debauched and pauperized the
nation. The wine experts dont explain to us that
Spain has been enriched: a country that never had

any drawback but its wine and the ignorance and vice that has always been allied with it. Spain has a national debt too, as large as ours and always increasing, and will doubtless never pay a cent of it.

PORTUGAL ETC.

Portugal, Italy, Hungary, Greece, Sicily are all wine countries and played out. They have supplied North and South America for a long time with beggars and bandits, drunken organ grinders, drunken fishermen, drunken sailors, drunken cooks, drunken shoe blacks and sometimes some very good people have come to us from Italy and perhaps some of the other countries named. These countries ought and no doubt would have been wealthy and prosperous in a very high degree but for their wine. They dont seem to have ever had any other drawback or obstacle but wine, and the ignorance, vice and pauperism which God decreed should be its inseparable companions. Our wine apostles dont write fulsome eulogies in the Chronicle and Bulletin and Record Union, calling the world's attention to the lofty, moral, social, political and financial eminence to which wine has raised Portugal, Hungary, Spain &c. They dont quite dare to do that, tho they have done bolder things in that line, trusting to the ignorance of their readers.

Peru is another country which has been very successful in making excellent wine and brandy; with a fabulous amount and variety of resources from guano, nitrate, silver, copper, cotton, alpaca and other wools &c, its wine and brandy, before the late war commenced, had pauperized the government and the country and sunk the people to the lowest depths of sensuality, debasement and imbecility. The wine sharps dont hold up Peru as a wine success, but they always say

FRANCE! FRANCE!! FRANCE !!!

Look at what a rich country wine has made France. Now if they can show that wine has ever added one dollar to the wealth of France without impoverishing France five dollars, the RESCUE will shut down from all further objection to the wine traffic and its enriching processes. But to say France is rich; France makes wine; therefore wine has made France rich, has exactly the same force as to say Messrs Stanford, Crocker, D. O. Mills, E. J. Baldwin, J. C. Flood are all rich men: they all have used wine; therefore, without doubt, drinking wine made them all rich.

Just exactly so we can say, England makes an enormous amount of beer, exports a little of it; England is rich; therefore beer has made England rich. Whereas beer and drink has made an enormous proportion of that most hardy and capable race, hopeless paupers, and has reduced five to ten times as many more to a condition more unhappy than that of a pauper fed at the public expense.

In next chapter the sources of the wealth and prosperity of France will be enquired into.

NUMBER IV

FRANCE AND ITS WEALTH.

It is proposed to look up the sources of wealth in France, to see how much drunkenness at home and the making of drunkards abroad, have contributed to that wealth.

The French people when sober are as careful, calculating, economical in all their modes of living as the Chinese; and they are probably as industrious as any other people in the world. Economy, industry, intelligence. sobriety, morality are about the sum of the sources of all national wealth. The lack of any one of these things is a leak in the national finances. In the two first, France stands first in the world, away ahead of all the rest. In the third she is among the foremost, and is not much behind any of her neighbors in the others. Therefore we have a reason good and sufficient, why France *ought* to be the richest. nation of Europe without any help from wine and brandy.

The French are the most intensely and practically patriotic people of the world. They never go out of France to spend a cent if they can help it. They never go abroad to display their wealth; never go elsewhere for pleasure: never buy anything foreign, if it can possibly be had, French. They believe a Frenchman, if he goes abroad to earn money, and dont intend to return and spend his fortune and himself, and live and die in France, is a rascal and a traitor. Reason No. 2 for being the richest people in the world.

The French have had a good land system ever since they guillotined their aristocracy in 1793. Great numbers of the agriculturists own their own farms, and none of them pay any rents to foreign absentee landlords. Reason No. 3 for prosperity.

France has a delightful climate and a most fertile soil, two important conditions of health, wealth and prosperity. It has abundant fisheries and employs vast numbers of ships and boats and men and boys in developing a wealth of food from that quarter. France has a splendid fleet of merchant ships and steamers, most economically and capably run by the most experienced and best trained and educated officers of the world, and the best navigators; far ahead of the American and English, as a class. France has a finely managed railway system and the attractions of its capital and its works of art and taste invite millions of tourists and travelers to come and squander there, the wealth they have earned elsewhere. That makes about six more sources of unusual wealth for France.

AND STILL MORE.

France has wood, coal, iron, salt, marble &c, almost every product of mine, field and sea that man needs. They manufacture almost everything, and here is an enormous source of *wealth*; for their manufactures are the most faithful and honest, and their material used the best in the world—in everything but wines and liquors; their people in that business could no more help being frauds than the English and Americans and Germans engaged in the same debasing, defrauding, destroying business.

The annual product of the silk, cotton, woolen and linen fabrics of France are about 640 million dollars and other industrial products amount to about 400 millions more. That is alone enough to make France wealthy without any other help.

France exports annually about 800 million dollars worth of material of which liquors are valued at about 45 millions. And here we can see most clearly the absurdity of claiming that any wealth is derived from her wine and brandy.

THE VINEYARDS

Of that country occupy about 3 ¾ per cent of all the lands, just the same amount as the public streets, roads, walks &c. The grape sugar product of this ground is converted into about 1000 million gallons of wine, of which about one seventh is made into brandy: 50 millions gallons are exported, valued at about 45 million dollars. The rest, 950 million gallons, value say 25 cents a gallon or 240 million dollars, is drank in France, and every one knows, that dont enrich France a particle. Not a whit more than burning 240 million dollars worth of powder would. But it pauperizes hundreds of thousands of people who drink it; drives them by thousands to jail, mad house, poorhouse, and suicide; every gallon of it that any one buys and drinks is a dead loss to him and is no more benefit to him than if he poured it on the ground.

DRUNKENNESS

Is appallingly prevalent and alarmingly on the increase in the wine and all the other districts of France. Immediately after the war with Prussia, stringent laws were enacted in France punishing drunkenness and a heavy fine was exacted of any barroom or restaurant, which had not a large printed placard hung up, specifying the penalties for drunkenness or selling liquor to drunks and minors.

In the Congress of France during the debate upon the enactment of that law, one of the members of that body declared, that in the portion of the French army that went to the war from his district, there was not a soldier who would not sit at a table and drink till he fell helpless under it, if he got the chance. "Mine is a district of light wines," said he, "gentlemen, and I challenge any of you to say that your soldiers were any more sober than ours," and no one disputed his assertion.

Perhaps it did not help to enrich France, that the drunkenness of her army led to their being soundly whipped, every time they were engaged with the Prussians; the latter sober because they were in an enemy's country and under stricter discipline.

Now while France exports the 45 million dollars worth of liquors, it is admitted there is money made by some of the exporters themselves, because a very large part of their export, all of it to North and South America and to most other countries—in fact about all the export, except a part of what goes to England, is only potato and apple alcohol and beet syrup whisky and water doctored. This wine costs them about 10 or 15 cents a gallon and sells for fancy prices, and there is a profit as well as a pleasure for the French wine doctor in gulling the poor silly wine guzzlers of Yankeedom.

This is no new thing, for there were regular premiums awarded at the Paris Expositions of 1855 and 1867 for fabricated wines.

A WASTE.

But let us now, after giving every credit to this wine, look at the debit side. To produce this wine for export and also to furnish material for more drink required by the people of France, vast imports are made of potato and rice and grain whisky from Holland, Belgium and Germany: British spirits from England; rum from the West Indies: and vast quantities of native beet sugar are made into spirits: so that it is somewhat doubtful if France after all, does not pay as much for her imports of beer and spirits as she gets for her exported drinks.

And a matter of much more consequence. Because of the waste of the ground employed in raising the grape sugar, to make this useless and pauperizing drink, France has to import over 200 million dollars worth of grain food for her people to eat, and of late years the balance of trade has been getting more and more against France every year: and because she utterly wastes all this land and labor devoted to the wine and brandy business, she has to pay out something like 200 million dollars a year in cash which never comes back. There is little doubt that the ground thus wasted would supply the food needed if properly used.

But for her wine, France would doubtless be incomparably richer than any other nation. But any impartial honest observer must see that that is her one weak spot, a cancer that is eating out the life of the nation. We have only looked at the financial question so far. But if the wretched and scandalously impudent falsehoods asserted as to the enriching effects of wine and brandy in France were true, what American would purchase national wealth at the price of the utter bandruptcy of American morals and decency ? Who covets the honor of supplying the world with harlotry and immorality and obscenity? Who covets to follow the example of one of the finest races and peoples the world has ever seen being transformed into a nation of libertines and drunkards ? and one whose population is decreasing under all conditions the most favorable for rapid increase, save this debauchery of wine.

And after preaching so long of the untold wealth that France derives from wine, the priests of Bacchus lately tell us, that this year (1881) because of the phylloxera, it must import 100 million gallons of wine to drink, about double their annual export. That is a confession that France must waste 250 million dollars worth of her own annual harvest in drink; then she has to pay 50 to 75 millions of cash to get more drink; and after that she must send money abroad to purchase 200 million dollars worth of bread which she might have raised upon her own vineyard lands that go to waste. This is bad economy and is pauperizing France by degrees.

But there is no wine that France will ever import, but the cheapest kind of Italian or other trash, that is not fit for market until it is doctored. It must be a wine that only the French would buy, and at a price that makes it about as cheap as the French fabricators can make from potatoes, thistles, beets, cider and molasses, which costs about 10 to 15 cents per gallon. The large "import of wine by France" is another delusion put forth by the wine sharps of this state to deceive the vineyard men.

ANOTHER MONSTROUS FABRICATION

was set afloat thru the Chronicle a few days ago to fool and deceive our vineyard men. It was stated that the transport of wine affords *about one-third* of the railway traffic of France. One-third of that traffic is about 20 million dollars; just enough to transport every gallon made in the country from the northermost to the southermost point of France and then back to where it started. But as it is probable not over one gallon in 20 goes any distance by rail or goes at all from the ranch on which it is made, it would have to pay 40 cents a gallon freight to pay one-third of the railway receipts. If the advocates of sobriety and prosperity, who desire to see grape growing make every vineyard man and every one of his family wealthy and happy, should assure them that a market is awaiting them for a millon tons of raisins every year in China at a dollar a pound, we would still have a larger margin of truth left us, than the wine and brandy sharps have ever presented as to that interest in other countries. Their impositions upon the farmers have been monstrous and cruel, like their business, which itself is the essence of fraud and wrong and mockery.

NUMBER V.

The question, does it pay or will it pay, to make this a wine and brandy country, is one of immense importance to Californians, but most of all, to the people who raise grapes. They, above all men, should look this question of *finance* square in the face, without prejudice or avarice or hate; they should weigh the matter intelligently, calmly, wisely. At the start they should drop forever, one gross mistake many of them labor under, which is that those who object to wine making are hostile to the welfare of the vineyard men. Look at the matter fairly, and see who is most likely to tell you the truth and be your friend. The one who has no axe to grind, no trade to make, does not ask a cent from you for any purpose whatever; or the party who is going to levy a commission and a profit and a shave on the wine and brandy you are coaxed to make, and the grapes you are to sell at his distillery?

Look at this matter squarely and you will see that two parties make each a separate proposition. The wine and brandy trader who expects to live and grow rich upon your toil, advises you to make wine and holds out the promise that a ton of your grapes shall be worth as much as a ton of Bodega potatoes, when there is a big crop of the latter, say $10 to $15 per ton.

We, the other party, who have not one cent of monied interest in the matter either way, propose to you to make a ton of your grapes, worth three or four tons of potatoes, as they really are and ought to be, three or four cents a pound at the vineyard. The wine maker's offer puts you and others too in deadly peril; our offer promises or threatens no harm to anybody. Can you refuse then to listen calmly and intelligently to a reasonable discussion of this matter? In the last article we were not quite done with

FRANCE.

Mr. Arpad Haraszthy tells you that you can always find a market in Bourdeaux for one hundred million gallons a year of California wine at 35 cents a gallon. Now if this is true, or if France would buy fifty million gallons even a year of our wine or any other wine, it forever gives the lie to the assertion made by the wine advocates, that wine and brandy-making, or either, is a profitable business for France. In the preceding number it was proved clearly that France owed nothing but loss and poverty to that business, but Mr Haraszthy confirms it when he says that France, after making 1,000 to 1,500 million gallons of wine, has to buy an enormous quantity in addition, for the use of her own drunkards.

And he supposes that to send this wine to France, the grapes from which it is made will be sold by the growers at $8 per ton (half the value of potatoes) which he thinks will pay a return to the millionaire capitalists, who he very properly supposes will have come to own all the vineyards by the time this State makes 100 million gallons of wine for export. He is right in implying that the wine making vineyards will change hands, as so many of them have done under mortgages and the bad management of those who use wine.

A recent article in the Chronicle (July 3rd) proclaims the fact too, that in the last 30 years the consumption of beer in France has been multiplied 43 times: has grown to be 43 times as much as it used to be. The increase of strong spirits we know is increasing in France and has been for 50 years at a terribly alarming rate; and it looks as if the wine business, which has pauperized every country that ever experimented with it, is fast having the same effect in France. The universal drunkenness which has ever followed wine in all countries is even too much for the frugal and ever economizing Frenchman, of whom it used to be said that 39 out of 40 were always hoarding a portion of their earnings, against one in five of the English.

About two years ago the wine advocates gave the following as the wine production of the world :

Countries.	Gallons.
France	1,505,000,000
Spain	528,000,000
Portugal	130,750,000
Italy	810,650,000
Austro-Hungary	57,300,000
Germany	156,900,000
Switzerland	10,460,000
Russia and Turkey	52,300,000
Greece and Cypress	26,150,000
Roumania	15,690,000
Total	3,806,200,000

Please look at it and decide if you please, which of those old wine producing countries you would desire California to resemble or copy, and in what respect if any.

Take from these countries the good and sober element that exists in France and Germany, and then the sober State of Maine, or the sober and christian portion of Massachusetts, or the grand State of Kansas, three States but a few days old in comparison with those countries—and the people of any one of them are of more importance to the world and exert a greater influence for good upon it and will continue to do so, than the whole of the others united. One vigorous young State of sober Christian American civilization is worth more than a dozen of these wine debauched, wine pauperized, wine benighted and wine brutalized nations.

And California has a future of wealth and power within her grasp, which can only be attained by a careful avoidance of the manifest pauperizing and barbarizing agencies to which is mainly due the present abject degraded condition of the miserable, despicable bankrupted and decayed nations who have prostituted their vineyards into a scathing curse to mankind.

GRAPES.

State aid and private aid, much individual enterprise and effort have been employed in originating and developing a wine and brandy system— under the mistaken idea that it was to become a paying business. But not a particle of effort, comparatively speaking, has ever been made to develop the grape business, the real business of the grape grower; the business God planned for us and gave us. Wine making is simply and only using the sugar in the grape, which can be had just as good and as useful and as cheap in the sugar cane, the cactus and the potato.

No society has ever attempted to create a market or instigate a snpply or develop a trade in canned grapes, in fresh pure wholesome grape juice, in grape jelly. Almost no energy has been put forth to stimulate a production of raisins and to secure a demand for our raisins and increase and advertize their excellence.

Not one intelligent effort has been made to secure a transport at honest figures for fresh grapes to the East, where there is a market for at least 1000 tons of fresh California grapes every day at 8 to 10 cents a pound, which ought to be divided in this way: freight 2½ cents; Eastern commission and expenses 2½ cents, and to the grape growers here, delivered at the cars, 3 cents per pound or more.

᾽ No effort has been made to abate the monstrous extortion of 6 or 7 cents a pound charged by the railroad companies where 2 cents would be an excessive rate to satisfy the most grasping monopolist on the Eastern side of the mountains. Not a protest has been made against the charge of seven cents freight on a pound of grapes which yields the grower one cent.

CALIFORNIA VITICULTURE.

The Commissioners appointed to supervise the drunkard factories and drunkard making interest of the state, have published their report, which states that the vintage of *"temperance material"* in 1880 was from 10 to 12 million gallons, thus—

    9,500,000 gallons Dry wines . . at 25 cents.
      700,000 gallons Sweet Wine . . at 60 cents.
      490,000 gallons brandy . . .   at $1.15

Which foots up to $3,312,500.

They also estimate the raisins at $100,000 and table grapes sold at $150,000.

Shipments from the State in 1880 were 2,487,353 gallons wine and 189,098 gallons brandy. Estimating these exports at the rates given above we have,

Value of wine exported . . . . . . $ 684,775
Value of wine for home consumption . . 2,110,225
Value of brandy exported 217,462
Value of brandy used as home temperance drink 300,038

                              ———————
                              $3,312,500

And we are treated thus to the information that to export $902,837 worth of drunkenness, we have to tax our own people to consume $2,410,263 worth of the same thing here, which is not only utterly useless, but which destroys the lives and properties of the people of the State, fills the country with murder, suicide, crime, divorce, debauchery and insanity, and is naturally and logically and inevitably the most pauperizing, demoralizing and destructive agency that ever cursed a country.

The *Chronicle*, reviewing the report, says: "Viticulture properly studied and managed, is within 20 years to become the leading industry of California, yielding a larger net revenue to cultivators than all other industries confined to the soil together."

This is quite possible for Viticulture; but it will be found an excellent policy for Viticulturists to plant such vines as will be most available, when in a very few years, the laws of the United States will make poison-wine and poison-brandy culture a criminal offence. And whenever that time comes the wealth and prosperity and peace and safety of the vine cultivator will be increased ten fold in the aggregate, and viticulture will be one of the happiest, most respectable and most profitable of accupations ever known.

The festive phylloxera is an inconvenient pest of the *grape farmer*, but it dont in the least incommode the *wine maker*. Altho it is said to have destroyed a million and a half of acres of vineyard in France, it has not reduced the volume of wine and brandy produced by one pint. As long as potatoes and rice and grain and beets and apples and molasses and sugar scrapings hold out all over France, Germany, Belgium, etc., they can produce any amount of precisely the same material as that from the rotted grape; the flavor only is a fabrication; the same water, the same alcohol from the same putrified sugar, the same sugar of lead and the same blue stone and drugs; and producing the same drunkenness and brutality.

In short, the fabrication of wine and brandy that sells for $5 and $10 and $20 a gallon, made from potatoes, thistles, cabbage, kitchen slops, swill-tubs, old boots and rags, drugs, etc., is rather to be commended for using a substitute and saving the wholesome grape for some useful purpose.

NUMBER VI.

GLUCOSE. A DISCOVERY ! ! !

The Santa Rosa Republican of Aug 4th 1881 has the following.

"It has leaked out that some dishonorable wine manufacturers in Napa Valley have imported Glucose for the purpose of adulterating wines. The Calistogian says:

"It is to be regretted that there are manufacturers of wine who are so grasping that they are not satisfied with the large profits already obtainable from pursuing their business in a legitimate manner—that there are men who will not hesitate to greatly injure an important business in this section of country, now being so prominently brought before the world, such prominence being due more to the purity of our wines than anything else."

The St Helena Vinicultural Society met and discussed the fraudulent undertaking, and denounced in a series of resolutions that mean business. One reads:

Resolved—That we, the St. Helena Vinicultural Association, condemn in the strongest terms any attempt by any party to adulterate our wine and brandy by the addition of any substance of whatever kind, and more particularly by the use of glucose, and that we will expose all parties importing or receiving the same, by publishing their names in the papers of this and the Eastern States, and that all wine dealers purchasing wine or brandies from winemakers using glucose shall also be published in like manner, etc."

Now what is Glucose ? some horrible, poisonous, villainous compound ? Not at all. It is simply grape sugar, precisely the kind of sugar found in grapes, figs and various sweet fruits. It is the only material in all those fruits that is of any use in the manufacture of wine or brandy: the pure water of the juice of course excepted. Most of the other varieties of sugar can be easily changed into Glu· cose; it exists naturally also in milk and eggs. and largely in honey. It can be chemically produced by the ton from starch and gum and other vegetable matters. Starch boiled in water that contains one per cent of sulphuric acid is in a very short time converted into glucose or grape sugar and only requires cleansing to be just the same. Diastase may be used also to convert starch into glucose: starch is an important per cent of the substance of potato, wheat, beans; various vegetables and all the cereals. Glucose may be made too from rags and some other materials when treated with sulphuric acid.

NO ADULTERATION.

It does not seem proper to call the use of glucose, in the manufacture of wine or brandy, an adulteration, for it is exactly the material from which grape wine is made. One man gets his glucose from rice, milk, honey, corn or potatoes; ferments it in water and produces alcohol and water, and a little flavoring extract being added, he has wine. The other man in Napa Valley subjects his grapes to exactly the same process of rotten putrefaction, which the decomposed body of a dead dog or cat has undergone when it is in its most intensely offensive and poisonous condition. The starch and nutriment and sugar and every good wholesome decent property of the grape, except the water, has

been destroyed. **Putrefaction has taken the glu-**
cose to pieces, separated its elements and put them
together in a new form, in which they have become
alcohol. That with the water and a grape flavor is
wine. Sugar, starch, gum, alcohol, and vinegar are
composed of exactly the same elements, but in
slightly varying proportions, and from starch or
gum all the rest can be made, but no alcoholic
liquor can be produced in any other manner than
by the putrefaction of glucose; and glucose is always
itself and the same, no matter how it is procured.

COMPETITION.

A great outcry is made by many persons and by
some temperance people too against adulteration
of liquors. Poisoning them with lead, strychnine
or vitriol is perhaps a little more wicked than poisoning them with alcohol. But the use of glucose
is only a competition of the potato and wheat-
grower with the vineyard men, and if the latter
will look at this matter rationally and practically,
they will see that at the start they are wofully
beaten and will be worse so every year.

The men who are importing glucose into Napa
Valley are proving that it is cheaper, imported
here, than grape sugar is raised in Napa Valley. If
that is so, how is it in England, Germany &c, but
more especially in the States east ol the Rocky
Mountains, where it is manufactured at a trifling
cost compared with its cost here. Will they ever
buy a dollars worth of *grape glucose* from Napa
Valley and pay freight on it, when they can produce at probably one third the price a precisely
similar article in their own cellars.

For many years one has seen "California Wine Depot" on the doors and windows and signs of cellars and stores and shops in any of the towns and cities all the way from the Missouri river to the shores of the Atlantic. Is there a single grape grower in California who is weak enough to believe that the wholesalers who have been for years supplying these *honest Depots*, have ever been silly enough to sell them a gallon of wine made in a California vineyard , when that would have cost them probably fifty cents or more a gallon, while they could make with their own glucose and "fixins" a superior article right on the spot at about 15 cents a gallon; possessing all the qualities of the genuine, just as good and as wholesome and so like, that the Californian himself, after turning round twice could not tell which of the two was his own.

The grape growers of California are never going to believe that the men who put up wineries and distilleries, are going to have the least regard for anything but their own pockets. No one will pretend that liquor dealers and makers can ever have the faintest scruples as to the manner in which they make money. They ought to know that every report made by them to our vineyard men about the prosperity of wine making countries and the condition of the wine making peasantry therein, has been utterly deceptive: they ought to know that these wineries and brandy makers hope to enrich themselves at the expense of the ruin of the properties and bodies and souls of the vineyard men: that they openly talk of peopling this State with a class of foreigners whose only recommenda-

tion is that they swill a swinish quantity of poisonous drink, which qualifies them to be stupid slaves
of the winery monopolist: that Chinese labor is to
do the vineyard and winery work and let the American children grow up hoodlums.

All this you grape growers know, and now when
every kind of the best wine and brandy can not only be fabricated in the cellars of San Francisco,
but can be made of the same quality in every respect from glucose &c, at about 15 cents or possibly
20 cents a gallon at the outside, do you suppose
these saintly dealers in drunkenness are going to
forfeit their chances of making the most they can
out of the folly of their customers, for the sake of
making *your* business profitable?

The competition is too much altogether for our
folks to stand. In France, Holland, Belgium, Germany, England, Jersey, Guernsey, Canada, and all
the States east of Kansas, in San Francisco,
Stockton, Napa, Sacramento, in every one of these
places they can make your wine and your brandy
out of cheaper material than you can raise from the
grape, and at prices that (if that was your
only resource) would soon put you in the same condition of beggary and serfdom and brutishness that
prevails among the winemaking populations of Europe, where a peasant's wages are at the highest 20
cents a day, one half payable in wine that has to him
no value whatever.

But there is not the least necessity for the grape
growers of California to become the plundered victims of their would be masters. With their ener-
gies directed aright, the grape devoted to its legiti-

mate honest uses, there is such a prospective
wealth in the vineyards of California,' as never
came to any agricultural system in the history of
the world. The grape used for wine purposes has
never profited anybody except an occasional "bloat-
ed capitalist:" it has blasted millions after millions.
But the grape always had and has now all the qualities
to make it the most enriching as it is the most beneficent and precious of all the food gifts of the Creator to man.

As a parallel to the glucose fraud, for it is a fraud
when its product is sold for more than 20 or 25
cents a gallon, the following is cut from the Wine
Dealers Gazette of July 1881.

THE ——— WHISKY IN PARIS.

. "We hope we are not intruding upon or into the
privacies of domestic life when we note the fact
that the agent of ——— the bonanza king, called on
Messrs ——— & Co., the agents of the ———
whisky and ordered shipped to Paris, one barrel and
ten cases of the "private stock," ——— brand, and at
prices that seem almost fabulous.

"No pent up Utica contracts our powers
For the whole boundless continent is ours,"

Thus it seems that Americans visiting Europe are
spreading the glad tidings of the superior quality
of the ——— whisky in foreign lands."

Now everyone who is posted on the subject knows
that that "private stock" of "fancy brand" and
"fabulous prices" is nothing more than common alcohol and water which costs per gallon, duty (perhaps) 90 cents—the alcohol itself 20 cents, flavoring
extracts 2 cents. And nothing else in the world

can be done to it to make it more valuable except to keep it a little while; and every appearance of age can be given it in 48 hours by a smart doctor. No doubt the millionaire of fabulous price and the Patrick Flanagan who wants the "cheapest and the wan that has the besht grip in it" have their wants supplied thru the same faucet and there are instances reported of a *private stock* of a "half barrel" of prime stuff just for our particular private friends, which has sent forth a continuous stream for the last 20 years and there are no symptons of it getting dry yet.

But the fancy prices for first quality whisky, brandy, and California wine dont go past the wholesalers who have cellars and buy glucose. But the wine grape growers will have to be satisfied to get $10 a ton for their grapes and rejoice at the luck of the people who get fabulous prices for the produce of their down cellar glucose vineyard.

Next thing to consider is how to make the grape profitable.

NUMBER VII.

There is one charge which can never be truthfully made against the advocates of temperance, They have never been known to destroy any man's business without making a better, more honorable and more profitable one open up before him. The destruction of the business of every individual who sold or made liquor in Maine or Kansas, made a better business possible for four or five men in place of it. And any one of those new possibilities was open to the saloonkeeper who wanted to reform and embrace an honorable means of livelihood.

It is so with the argument against wine and brandy making: we warn the vineyard men against making themselves helpless slaves of the glucose wineries and distilleries; against wasting their grapes for $10 a ton as they will soon have to, if no resource is open to them but the wine vat: but all the damage and wrong we propose to do them is to point them to $50 or $60 or more a ton. and that too, in a business as reputable and honorable and happy and healthful and pleasant as the world can show elsewhere.

But to do this requires something more than paper talk, or expressions of opinion. A very great activity has been put forth in the past by a few interested individuals who were anxious to rope in the vineyard men to raise wine grapes, to enrich the big wineries and distilleries and glucose dealers, at the expense of the pauperization and ruin and damnation of the vinegrowers who could be induced to become their dupes. A similar activity exercised by the vinegrowers in a legitimate direction will produce beneficent results, in place of the disasters planned by the speculating operators who have engineered the Viniculturist schemes.

THE C. P. R. R.

We hear of California pears and peaches selling in the East at such fabulous prices as indicate that the great bulk of the people there, are prohibited from ever purchasing more than a rare taste of them. A few years ago the people of Vineland were complaining bitterly that they could not at times get over five cents a pound for their grapes, during the most plenteous state of the market and they were afraid it would get worse. At the same time people here were selling them at $8 to $15 a ton for wine.

If there were only a half dozen carloads a month or year, the R. R. Co, would be justified in charging an extra freight for the extra trouble incurred in their management. But when they can afford to bring certain classes of freight from New York to San Francisco at $25 per ton—when they talk of carrying the wheat crop of this State to Galveston and Liverpool for something like $15 a ton, when we know that freight is customarily $3 a ton from Chicago to New York, nearly one third the distance from here to New York,—we know that the R. R. Co can make large money by carrying 1000 tons of grapes and other fruit a day at 2 or 2½ cents a pound quick freight, and that there would bo a ready sale for that amount every day at prices which would leave 3 or 4 cents a pound to our grape and fruit growers and for choice qualities much more.

It is of no advantage to the Cailfornia fruit grower to know that 3 Cal. peaches or pears sell for 25 cents in New York, for all it amounts to is, that the railroad millionaires have made a net profit of nearly $1,000 a car load, the speculator who took the risk has made $200 or $300 if he had good luck in preserving his fruit, and one or two fruit growers have got a cent or two a pound for small lots, in place of 500 of them selling one or two tons apiece at good rates every morning of the season.

Of course the railroad managers would much prefer to carry 100 tons of merchandise in a given time for $20,000 net profit, than to carry 500 tons in the same time for the same amount of net profit, even if at the latter rate they were realizing a return of 25 per cent a year upon their capital. It is less trouble for them and they consult the interest of no one else. A reduction in freight upon grapes may foreshadow to them a general reduction upon other merchandize, therefore they are not likely to propose it

In a very short time, were any reasonable rate of freight offered for fruit hence to the East, we should doubtless arrive at a method of packing and preparing it, so as to insure its arrival in prime condition always: in that case the demand for our grapes in the Eastern market would for a long series of years, keep ahead of our capacity to supply, and thus highly remunerative prices would be maintained.

An important consideration just here is that our fruit sent East will never in the least reduce the capacity of our customers there to purchase from us next year and for twenty or fifty years to come. On the contrary the generous use of our wholesome fruit will be an assurance of their continued health and ability to continue good, paying customers. Not so with the brandy and wine; a large proportion of our present customers or rather consumers of these things, will in a short time be in the poor house, in the gutter, in the penitentiary and our future sales must depend upon the ensnaring of fresh victims to their ruin. There is no denial that can be truthfully made to this: but we do not deny either that some of the customers and consumers of wine and brandy and some of the makers too, will get along pretty soberly, live to a good age and maintain a well deserved reputation thruout for being good hearted, generous, kindly, honest, obliging characters. First rate fellows in every thing but one: one fault or misfortune they certainly have in the matter of drink.

MORE RAILROADS.

A business of transportation which would improve very largely the annual revenues and the actual capital value of every farm and property of this State is of many million times the importance that the gabble about greenbacks and the cooperation of drunken working men, and the Chinese and communist questions are, all of which could be settled by the instant prosperity that a prohibitory law would give us. And a railroad project that would reduce to one third of their present amount the fares and freights paid by the people of the State and thus enormously increase the business and wealth of the people, is a subject well worthy of the most elaborate consideration and discussion.

Evidently the easiest and best solution of all the complicated questions, between the railroads and the people would be the building by our general government of a trunk line from Atlantic to Pacific. We should never want any other regulation of freights and fares, nor any more railroad commissions paid by the people to sell out the people. There can never be a valid objection offered to such a project, that does not apply with equal force to a government postal service, which is an inestimable public advantage and has no objectionable drawbacks.

Our farmers and fruitraisers and our citizenship should actively set this project in motion with a determination to win. And in the meantime every aid and encouragement should be tendered by the State to the pushing of rival lines from Eastern connections to the Pacific. These would help to break down the present enslaving and grinding monopoly, which not only exacts such a merciless tribute from the industries of the State, but which notwithstanding many advantages afforded by it, has kept in force a stringent tyrannical ukase which paralyzes a vast agricultural interest with a 7 cent freight on a 1 cent product. The freight of a ton of paper worth $220 here is $25 from New York.

The freight of 1 ton of grapes worth here $20 to $25 is $140 to New York.

The most important financial question that ever came before the fruit raisers of the State is, how can we get our product shipped to the East and be permitted to participate in the profits of its sale.

NUMBER VIII.

It has been heretofore stated in these articles, that the vine growers have been purposely misled by parties interested in deceiving them. Some of these have had grape lands to sell, and have clothed a ruinous, pauperizing, despicable, drunkard breeding interest in a stolen garment of gold and purple, to defraud ignorant men into paying fabulous prices for the lands they wished to get off their hands or to sell for others at a round commission. Others have had grape cuttings in great variety to sell and have sought to induce innocent cultivators to plant the worthless kinds that are suitable only for wine, and will not make raisins. Then winery owners desire that large crops of grapes shall be at their mercy at $8 or $10 a ton, as they soon will be, when of no use but for wine. And then the wine and brandy merchants want to buy their wine at 15 or 20 cents and sell it for 50 cents or a dollar. All who advise the pushing of the wine business, are going to sell something, or make something out of the vine growers, and have a private money making reason of their own for urging the falsehood that it is a profitable business, whereas, they know it has debauched and pauperized and unmanned every people that have ever engaged in it since the time of Noah.

And now let us listen to the admissions of a wine expert who has a very strong interest in promoting the manufacture of wine for him to sell. Mr. A. Harazsthy compares the extravagant results paraded by the owners of large tracts of grape lands before the eyes of cultivators, with the practice of salting mines to help their sale. He says any one planting a vineyard and expecting more than $30 or $40 an acre from it, will be disappointed and anything over $40 ought to be considered a golden harvest. The RESCUE has often declared that grapes for wine would be sold at $10 or $12 a ton at soon as the furor of 1880 has subsided. Mr. Harazsthy says that in five years they will go down to $7 or $8 a ton, and the cask may cost more than the wine is worth, as it has been in France owing to the large production. But he still says we can always find a market for wines in Bordeaux at 35 cts a gallon delivered there. And he expects that in our southern states a splendid market will be always found for California wines.

The fact that France raises 1000 to 1500 million gallons of wine a year, and exports about 50 million gallons and drinks all the rest, and after that enormous waste of land and labor and capital, is now purchasing vineyards in Hungary, Germany and Italy, and buying up spirits made from potatoes, beets, turnips, glucose and sugar, in Germany, Belgium and Holland, and oceans of beer and gin from England, with which to fabricate wines and brandies and absinth, to supply the inordinate cravings of her many millions of insatiable drunkards during the few years of short grape harvests, and is ready to buy 100 million gallons of wine a year from California—ought to be a full and complete answer for ever, to the monstrously and manifestly absurd proposition that wine and brandy making could ever be profitable to the country or people that engage in it.

Mr. Harazsthy says very truly that Eastern dealers will only buy the cheapest wine from us, and will only buy cheap while they are selling dear. Therein lies an immensely important fact to the vine grower; any Eastern wine dealer who knows the business, can buy the very cheapest wines that are made in the state at the lowest price, and out of that same cask he can sell in three days after, the very finest quality of wine produced anywhere, that the producer cannot tell from his own. And without having added more than a cent or two a gallon to its cost, he sells it at the top fancy price. Those who do not know that fact are blind.

And there is one very imposing future obstacle to the wine interest, but it will be the greatest blessing which could come to the vinegrowers; in a very few years, altho now they pretend to ignore it, the sale of any of the poisons manufactured from the rotted, prostituted grape will be a serious criminal offence all over this Union and the civilized world.

This subject has been treated altogether from the financial or commercial standpoint. Nothing has been said at all of the hideous criminality of turning this beautiful state into a shambles of drunkenness, vice, violence and unlimited debauchery.

NUMBER IX.
Adulteration of Wine. [1883]

Interesting revelations of fraud in making French wines have recently startled the public and the drinkers, altho the trade and the temperance experts have known for 30 years that every kind of alcoholic liquor, from the highest to the cheapest, is cheaply counterfeited and fraud is the general rule everywhere.

The municipal authorities of Paris recently analized 3,361 samples of French wine. Only 387 were pronounced good, 1063 passable, and 1,911 were declared BAD. And this was done by experts favorably interested toward the wine trade of their country. A Paris correspondent of the *Chronicle* (J. H. H.) writes that France produced from 1868 to 1878 an average of 1,320 million gallons of wine, but since then only an average of 550 millions, because of the phyloxera.

But there has been all along as much used in France and as much exported as ever. In 1881 France imported 176 million, made 132 million from raisins and press refuse, and 264 million gallons more from all sorts of substitutes, the latter flavored often with poisonous ingredients, beside the alcohol in it.

The dealers of San Francisco import cases, bottles, corks and labels from France, and sell the wine they put in them as French. No harm done beyond the falsehood of the label. One is as good and will make drunk as well as the other, and the .poor silly buyers who think it high-toned and European to drink the trash, can only judge of the quality by the price.

It is most important to our vineyard men to remember that the French, English and all others who *deal* in alcoholic drinks always can and do make imitations cheaper than the genuine. So if any quality of Cal. wine should ever bring a fancy price, the city cellar vineyard will make it and rake in the profits—not the grape growers. And the cheap fraud made from glucose, potatoes and pulque-cactus is just as good as the genuine.

HOW IT PAYS FRANCE.

After centuries of wine growing, and the world for a market, a short crop compels France to expend an enormous sum to satisfy the depraved appetites of her people with imported and fabricated poisons, that would be vastly more profitable to the nation if they were all poured out into the sea; or if the money, time and labor had been employed in making and burning firecrackers.

Let us figure up the wine account of France.

Cost of 550,000,000 gals. genuine wine produced at 15c			$82,500,000
" " 176,000,000 " imported wine at 15c			26,400,000
" " 132,000,000 " made from refuse and raisins at 10c			13,200,000
" " 264,000,000 " imitation wine at 10c			26,400,000
1,122,000,000			$148,500,000
deduct 50,000,000 " exported, say at 90c			45,000,000
Money, time and labor wasted			$103,500,000
Add to this the value of the imported bread which might have been raised on the grape lands, 7,000,000 acres			120,000,000
Annual money loss by wine			$223,500,000

To this vast waste in a thing utterly useless, we might add 500 million dollars a year more, for the damage to the nation in idleness, vice and crime caused by wine; a very low estimate. It does not matter if these statistics are inexact; if they are 25 or 50 per cent. too high or too low, the fact remains that the business is an enormous pauperizer. Throw off 100 or even 200 of the 223 millions and it is still ruinous. Imagine for fancy's sake that the 223 millions were money profit, that would not begin to compensate the misery, madness, crime and ruin made by the infernal curse of poison wine.

CONCLUSION.

Temperance men have never tried to hurt a man's business without giving him a choice of at least five better ones which would be open to him if the drunkard and pauper making industry were abolished.   We now earnestly warn our grape growers to guard in time, against the coming evil day when their wine grapes at $8 and $10 a ton, will throw their lands and homes into the hands of the big winery monopolist and counterfeiter, who will in time gobble up all his small neighbors.   We warn them against the 1,000 to 10,000 acre vineyards, with no church, no school, no homes but a few rickety slave huts, occupied by Mexican, Chinese or Indian savages.

٭ We point them to a brighter picture of the future which we ask them to paint for themselves.

When in the near future a carload of fresh grapes shall be carried to the East and North for $120 to $160 or $15 or $20 a ton freight as they surely will, this State will find a ready paying market for 1,000, 2,000 even 3,000 tons of luscious table grapes to go East every morning, if they can produce them; and the demand for raisins and canned fruit and probably fresh grape juice prepared in wholesome wine, can never be supplied.   Thus we shall distribute a daily nourishing wholesome blessing among our brethren all over the continent, and at the same time reap for ourselves a seven fold profit over any result possible from wine.   How infinitely better than to send abroad a blasting curse to turn our country into a den of sin, barbarism, misery and ruin, like the pauper wine countries of the old world.

Our picture of the future puts on every 1,000 acres of vineyard 50 to 100 happy American homes of virtuous, well-paid industry, nurseries of intelligent worthy citizenship, with churches, schools and every requisite of the noblest civilization. That is the way we desire to harm the grape growing business.   This is too good a country to be turned into a nursery of pauperism and vice.

www.ingramcontent.com/pod-product-compliance
Lightning Source LLC
Chambersburg PA
CBHW030907260626
47169CB00008B/2723